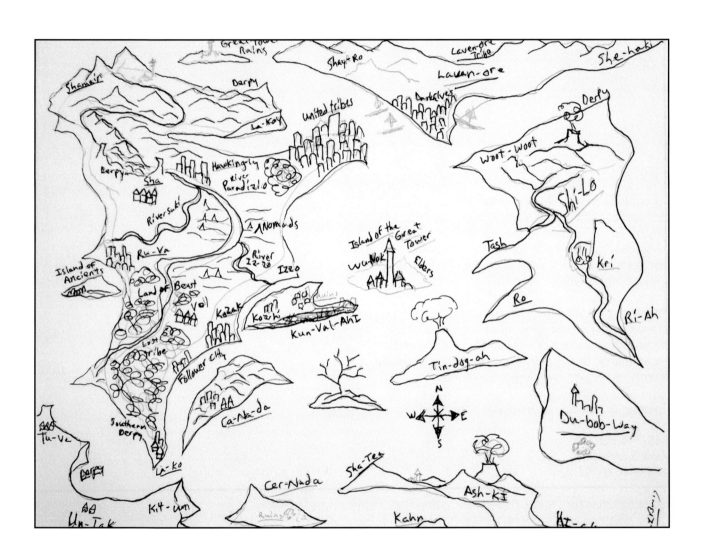

To order additional copies of this book, contact:
Xlibris
844-714-8691
www.Xlibris.com
Orders@Xlibris.com

ISBN: Softcover   978-1-6698-0308-9
        EBook   978-1-6698-0309-6

Print information available on the last page

Rev. date: 12/09/2021

THE BOOK OF THE BIRDS VOL:1

The Tribes of Parlo-5

Jacob Bucy

The Book of the Birds Vol:1 The Tribes of Parlo-5

A long time ago in a forgotten and ancient part of the universe hides a small galaxy with eight planets. It is not quite known how old the Parlo system is. But its fifth planet is a quirky and mysterious one to say the least. This is where our story begins on the continents of Parlo-5 and the curious societies that have formed there. Teaming with life of various sorts, from elves, changelings to an abundance of species of bird like creatures. There are over 50 tribes and 8 major natation's on Parlo-5. We will start on its largest and most populated continent Paradiz-io. This continent is home to many flocks, gaggles, and tribal societies. The largest and most domineering of the tribes are The United Tribes of the Eastern Front. Led by king Uzz-ssahh, and his Cryptor of power. King Uzz-ssAHH dream is to unify all of Parlo-5 and have a one world government and gives promises of ridding parlo-5 of predatorial threats, bring peace, trade, currency and a more structured place for all to enjoy. Though this thought makes Uzz-ssahh smile many obstacles stand in his way. The tribes of Paradiz-io have been wearing with each other for 50 lunar cycles. King Val-ziah of the Hawking-ly tribe has been sending out raid parties and giving threats' of expanding their kingdom. It is also rumored the Hawking-ly still consume the flesh of their enemies'. King Val-ziah is not the only king with potential genocide on their hands. King uzz-ssahh has sent out parties to the north and nearly irradicated all of the Shamain tribe in the North West Territory. Uzz-ssah plans to hold a conference and welcome leaders and representatives of all the tribes to a conference to ask them to join and embrace his vision and establish his dominance. Uzz-ssahh is furious with several that have outwardly expressed their discontent and refusal to attend his gala of disaster. The criticism drives the king blinding mad. One of his hopes another larger group has started converting the flocks and tribes in the south of Paradiz-io to their theistic ideas, and their leader known as the Great Old One has already expressed his gratitude and sent gifts to the arrogant Uzz-ssaHH. What Uzz-ssahh does not fully realized the great old one and his followers of the great spirit have an agenda of their own and veil many secrets amongst their society. King Val-ziah has sent his sons and their legions and warriors on separate missions while keeping a fierce some force to protect his city of Val. Tutor is heading north and Hero is heading east towards the capital of the united tribes of the eastern front. In the south some of the tribes have been teaming up some have been massacred.

The Tribe of Izzo has been the most aggressive and disruptive. They reject Uzz-ssah, hunt the Derpy of the south and plan to take the lands of their enmities and neighbors. But in recent years the followers of the great spirit have been at the top of their list of vengeance. In the past Izzo have fought alongside the Hawking-ly and have the same taste in meat. Hero hopes to help Izzo and re kindle the friendship between the two tribes and take over capitol city. What hero is unaware of 50 lunar cycles of war and shortages in harvest have impacted the populations in the south. Some claim even plagues are wiping out the smaller and more feeble flocks.

From the north Tutor sends word to his father of the destruction he is finding in the aftermath of the genocide of the Shamain. Tutor hopes to get the smaller flocks of nomadic tribes to join and fight alongside the Hawking-ly. Tutor is depressed at the notion that the Nomadic tribe's leader rejected his invitation. His reasoning is his tribe is peaceful and interacts on a friendly basis with all of Parlo-5.

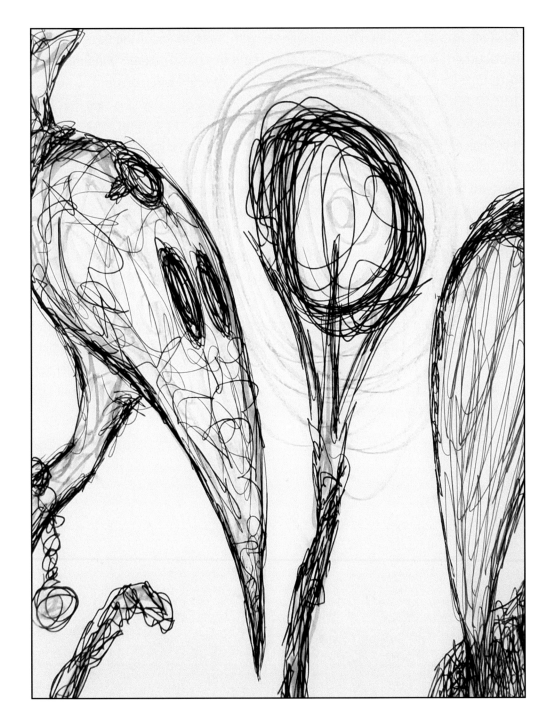

While paradizzio was in turmoil from war, issues with trade, much of the nuts, fruit and vegetables, the birds in the southern hemisphere watch and plot. The tribes of un-tuk are banding together with the khan plotting to take over shil-lo and todoggah. The bearded one leader of the Kri, he is among those sensitive to the energies and changes that are seemingly growing by the day. It is said that the Bearded one is as old as the watchers another descendent of the ash-ka-wii tribe the original inhabitants of Parlo-5. He warns the Kri council of his premonitions, but they did not take him seriously and many were planning on attending the banquet and meetings with the United Tribes of the Eastern Front. Little did the bearded one know; this would be the last time he sees the council together and will have to take on a leadership role. The derpy tribes have all refused to go to the gathering instead are preparing for their annual pilgrimage to the ancient island. There they will regroup and see who are the survivors. Throughout parlo-5 the birds are ever increasingly anxious. The civil wars in paradizio are taking their toll. Regular raids from the Elves and the Hawking-ly not to mention the food shortage the flocks, tribes and creatures of all walks are being affected and are worried of what is to come.

King Uzz-ahh is gathering more troops increasing security, adding curfews in capitol city, as well as other major cities across ParadiZzio. Many of the tribes and communities try to fight back but only to have their homes destroyed or become victims and casualties of this ongoing war over territory, trade, and power. The king has hired an assassin to carry out some dirty work on few tribes that Uzz-ahh deems as threats to the agenda he has placed into order.

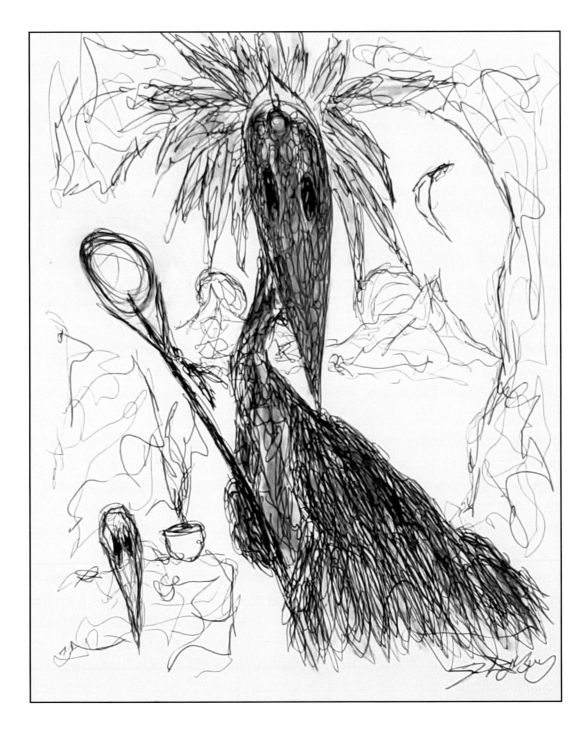

In the north Tu-tor and his legions put up a good fight against the massive army of the united tribes. Hero and the Izzo are making their way to capitol city. A jetti- hawk but the name of Sak-er notifies Uzz-ahh of the approaching army. He summons for the northern army to return to the city. Tu-tors whereabouts are unknown. Many of tu-tor's army fell that bloody day. What few survivors ended up as prisoners of war. Hero un-aware of what has happened in the north charges onward. Often at stopping points he gives speeches to his warriors and Izzo's army. He boasts about the Hawking-ly's plans to govern Paradizio and stories of his families' early days and claim to the hawking-ly throne. On the third day they arrive at the capitol city. 5miles away from the city and Hero notices a massive army waiting for them. Hero and Izzo look at each other with concern. Hero then turns and dose the call for the troops to charge.

Uzz-ahh had waiting for Hero's arrival 3 massive armies, the battel lasted for hours but the sheer numbers of the United army were simply too much for the hawking-ly and the Izzo. Uzz-ahh sits gazing to his scepters and thinks about his speech he will give at the meeting that is quickly approaching. So far, many tribes have responded and will be there. Though his power is growing with increasing numbers by the day, much of Paradi-zzio is dying. The next day would be the day he meets with the leaders of Follower City. Cera, Seedrick and Tia eagerly await the meeting. Meanwhile to no-ones knowing the great old one and his students have been practicing ancient rituals affecting all of Parlo-5. Many species across Parlo-5 have died off due to famine and drought. The king's popularity beginning to fade.

Sutto studied much with the elders and has embarked on a journey to visit and study the ruins of Paradizz-io in hopes of finding more crystals and objects that may help him travel back and prevent the destruction of the Shamain. Days turn to weeks as he travels, but at last in a secluded temple ruin he finds a glowing sphere as he touches it a surge of energy fell over him. Now all Suto has to do is to find a light post that will allow him time travel. In the old temple an ancient tablet warns of the effects of time travel on the mind and body. But much of the tablet had been destroyed. Sutto did not care he was going to save Parlo-5.

Du-bo the wise has been watching the alignments of the stars and moons he fears that soon the conditions will be right for whom ever is practicing the ancient magic to become stronger. Du-bo reaches into a satchel and pulls out his power crystal and begins attaching it to a staff. He warns the Derpy not to attend the conference and banquet but to rally the surviving Derpy tribes and be ready to defend themselves. Du-bo sets off in search of his brothers. He travels north to the northern coast where he plans to go to Laven-Ore to find Hermit and then hopes the two of them will find Sutto and find him alive. The Shamain brothers are thought to be quite powerful. For they are a mixture of species bird and unknown. The Shamain though had always had a deep connection to spirit and the elements. There are several crystal spheres mainly tribal leaders wield them. The Shamain's sphere belongs to Du-bo, he had given an oath he would use it wisely and protect it. When Du-bo received this powerful gem, he was warned that one day there will be a quest to unite all the spheres and change the world as they knew it.

The Hermit after receiving a sphere from a watcher is heading south to reunite with his brothers. It will take the three of them, to stop those responsible for the chaos affecting Parlo-5. Hermit being the eccentric that he is left the Shamain many years before the raids began. He wanted so badly to be alone, no longer teach and he lost his faith in spirit. He reminisces about his youth and his lessons. He remembers an old tale of magic destroying planets and of the Maker, the one who made many of the objects of old that possessed many abilities and power. The Hermit during his time on Laven-ore became friends with an unlikely ally but one who also fears and notices the planet is in trouble. Ki-ev offers to join Hermit on his journey. The cantankerous Hermit wishes him well but will not accept the offer. By night fall Hermit makes a fire and dose a ritual to seek the council of spirits. In a trance like state, he gazes into the smoke and sees the silhouettes of his ancestors and spirits who watch over him. They warn of the threats and warn that if he fails this mission Parlo-5 will be in grave danger and that the Hermit must convince the tribes to ban together to stop the threats to their beloved planet.

The Ash-ki-ow-ie were the original bird species that inhabited Parlo-5. It is said that from them all birds were formed. No known survivors of this ancient flock. It was said the Primal bird's leader shiz-ka is the oldest living bird on Parlo-5 with the royal watcher being the only one older. The watchers are the mystical and mythical creatures that watch over parlo-5. Some say it was them who made the Ash-ki-owie. The Primal birds are thought to be the eyes for the watchers. The watchers have no eyes, they feel everything. Many believe their feathers especially the tail feathers of the Royal watcher have magical abilities and powers. After the primal birds more and more species spread across the planet from corner to corner. Another ancient and abundant creature were the Derpy and the Shamain. The Derpy's numbers are dwindling and Shamain thought to be extinct the future looks bleak for these tribes. If you were to ask some, they would point to the alignment of the 2 suns the crescents moon. These believers of the old ways are few and far now however they been warning any and all who would listen of great changes and dire circumstances approaching.

The watchers learned of the news of the banquet and meetings of all the tribes in capitol city and are worried. After gathering in the great tree few got together around the fire pit and focused their thoughts to see what is out of balance and spiraling out of control on their cherished planet. One watcher took it upon himself to try to warn the tribes and to find out what is happening. Many of the watchers fear old magic is responsible for the planet is out of balance and food shortages are starving much of parlo-5. The watchers all gather in a great and old tree. The Royal watcher in the middle stresses they are not to interfere. The watcher known as zykk, did not agree with the royal watcher's wishes. H decides to make it his duty to save Parlo-5 he will approach a good friend to seek his help. Hermit to convince him to go on a dangerous journey to find out and stop whatever is going on beyond the sight and feelings of the watchers. Technically the watchers took an oath to never to interfere but to only look out for the planets best interest and warn of threats coming from the stars. Zykk stresses to the Hermit he must succeed and prevent catastrophe and disaster from continuing. Three other watcher's know and agree with Zykk's plan to investigate and stop whatever is going on causing the balance of an entire world to shift into chaos and famine.

The Hermit is among three known survivors of the Sha-main tribe north of the canyon. Tutor and his army destroyed, enslaved, and burnt all of what the three Brothers knew. The Sha-main brothers are cantankerous and quirky sorts. Hermit only speaks to a select few a couple times a year. His twin brother Suto is very outgoing, and his oldest brother Du-bo the wise is often feared and thought to of lost his mind. When the village fell Hermit went north to Lavan-ore Du -Bo to the canyon and Suto fled to the Island of the Great Tower. During his time in Lavan-ore Hermit spent many days searching for old ruins and relics from a forgotten past. He thinks of his brothers often and sobs for those he lost. He however finds comfort in his solitude. On the third day of the 7th cycle the watcher finds Hermit. Zykk begins to tell Hermit everything. Hermit was not amused by the news at all. In his words "let it all burn." After arguing and pacing back and forth Hermit realized he must do this for his friend and for Parlo-5.

The Sha-main, often served on royal courts, teachers, prophets, and even healers. But over time they became shunned cause they did not think, act or even fully resembled other species. It is unclear why they were targets of prejudice and misconceptions. The Sha-main is endangered and on the verge of being extinct. Suto arrived on the Island of the Great Tower and found one of his teachers there. She knew of his arrival and only wished it was better circumstances. The three brothers studied with the elders on the island for majority of their lives. They studied ancient languages and texts. They learned of fables and mysteries and curiosities that shroud Parlo-5. Suto is bent and determined to somehow save his flock. He immediately goes into the tower and heads inside the library where he begins research on some relics that may be of some use. The outgoing Suto on his stay on the researched and studied and pondered all sorts of mysteries and tales, but when he learned of special lamps and lanterns that would react to power crystals, he became obsessed. One such the watcher's lantern can transcend time and space to any destination any time period, but at a cost. It appears one must use extreme caution when traveling through time this way. Without proper tools it can deform and even cause death of the one who powers the lantern.

Du-Bo the wise went to the canyon where he stayed with the few remaining Derpy in the caves. Du-BO yearns to hear word from his love Nok, he last saw her before she left to go to Tindogah to study the power crystals that can be found on the island's volcano. Du-Bo Plans to go with the Derpy to their annual pilgrimage and find out how many are left and to rally them against the Uzz-ahh and Tutor to have their revenge. Du-bo steps outside, one can still feel the tense and charged air flowing through the canyon. As he gazed upon the horizon, he noticed the formation that the lunar cycles were on is exactly as an elder prophecy to him when he was just a chickee. The next morning Du-Bo said good bye to his friends and set out to go to capitol city for the Banquet and gathering king Uzz-Ahh is throwing. He plans to rally the tribes to revolt and stop this madness that was falling upon their beloved planet. Late that night a watcher came to Du-Bo and handed and handed him without word or warning a septor with a glowing crystal mounted at the end. The watcher stood in total silence, but Du-Bo knew exactly what to do.

The next morning the suns and the crescent moon glisten in the sky. Du-bo sends a message to Hermit via primal bird for him to meet with him at capitol city in two days. Along the way towards the north to find Hermit he realized the Banquet and conference was only days away and that if he could rally support, he just may be able to stop the peril plaguing the planet. He knows the time is almost right for the veil to be thin enough that those whom studied the magical arts will be more powerful.

The day of the banquet has arrived and the conference to be the following day. Du-bo sees the capitol city skyline appear. Du-bo has never seen such a sight. Also arriving at capitol city Hermit remembers the knowledge he gained in the ruins on Laven-ore and the criticism of its tribe that he attempted to warn of the impending doom. Hermit learned tails of the great wars of the seventh cycle of the new moon that caused the tribes to be divided and of the turmoil among the tribes of Laven-ore. Hermit fears history may repeat itself if they fail to find out and stop whomever is behind the chaos. Near a caffe Hermit sees his brother and the two are happy to see each other. Du-bo is shocked that his brother seems to be changing. Changing for the good as they talk of where their journeys have taken them. Hermit warned Du-bo that the tribes of Laven-or may not be of help at least at this time. Laven-ore is a harsh environment between rugged terrain, harsh weather patterns, and tribes that may be the most temperamental and fierce of any on Paradi-zio. Du-bo was appalled when he learned of Hermits alliance with the Elves and his friendship with Kiev. The Elves are among the birds' worst enemies. Hermit re assures Du-bo that the Elves have suffered as the Birds. The elves have been affected by plague nearly wiping them all out. Many elves have retreated to the caverns below Laven-ore. Du-bo not convinced of the change in heart of the elves sits attentively listening to the stories of Hermits adventures.

The night before the banquet the king met with the representatives from Follower city, he discussed his plans with Cera and Seedrick over dinner. Little did he know that it is the followers affecting the planet and had a hidden agenda to de throne the king. Seedrick assures the king him and his fellow priest will do their part to ease his burdens while Cera agrees to send one thousand troops to aid the Kings army in convincing the tribes who do not attend the conference.

The morning of the banquet Du-bo met with a watcher who had come to warn him for him and the Hermit to flee the city and return to the canyon. At the canyon they will be re united with Suto. The watcher warned that Suto was in grave danger. That they should convince him to join with them and finishing their task of saving Parlo-5. Capitol City is extremely crowded with all who have attended and spectators from far and wide have filtered in to hear from their delegate. As they travel in and out of the back-alley ways trying to avoid any of Uzz-ahh's army the noticed in the far-off distance the astrological alignment is just like what the Hermit described to Du-Bo and it would appear that the prophecy is true and about to come into fruition.

Suto as he crests a hill has found the temple of time. Armed with his sphere, lantern and new found knowledge he hopes to learn more about time travel. The last scroll that Suto read talked of a crown that the maker had made that was stolen by a young boy from another world who came to Parlo through a portal to one of the lamps at the gates of the Temple of Time. The crown is supposed to protect one from the radiation and extreme stress that one receives while time traveling. As he inters the temple, he sees glyphs everywhere and he sees two lamp posts approximately ten feet apart. Some of the murals on the wall in the main chamber show a crown glistening and studded with gems that appear to be power crystals and it shows the lantern. Suto thought to himself if this is his lantern, find the crown and travel back by opening the portal at the temple of time. As he continued to explore Suto found the temple library. He sat down to take it all in, he sobbed with tears of joy that he may be able to save his flock. Suto realized there would be a chance that the boy king may still be alive and roaming Parlo-5 and that the Maker may also be here. The Maker tired of the squabbling, politics, and mis use of the things he crafted and gifted to the tribes he left for a self-exile but his ware bouts are unknown. When the primal bird with the message from his brothers found Suto, the message from his brothers made him cry. Armed with a sphere, power crystal necklace, and lantern he must find the crown. Suto however did head the call of his brothers and set out for the gorge in the northern part of Paradi-zio. Against better judgement he walked up to the two-lamp post waved the sphere and held the lantern and stepped forward into a portal.

The banquet seemed to be a success but the conference was where the king felt most pressure for half of those there were there in support others were either in disagreement or indecisive on where they stood. In his speech he talked about those issues plaguing Parlo-5. Drought, famine, plagues, war, and predators feeding upon the weak. He proposed for there to be a universal currency one that would benefit all the tribes. He then had his attendants pass out coins that bared the crest of the United Tribes of the Northeastern front and on back a likeness to King Uzz-ahh. Many were appalled by the arrogance, and not willing to change. The Suki delegate stood and criticized the king and announced that the seeds, furs, and goods that are bartered have already been established why change now. The king glared with frustration, and pointed out that the great flowers that produced the seeds were cultivated by a tribe who was too good to attend the conference and drought is causing production of seeds to fall. Uzz-ahh and his supporters feel that a one world government with a universal currency would be beneficial to all and for the first-time trade with the flocks on other continents could be established for the first time since the great wars of the seventh cycle of the new moon. Many rejoiced and cheered for the king, this only fed the arrogance from the king. As he turned, he whispered to one of his attendants to have the Suki delegate "taken care of." The tindoghan, kri, and un-tuk all had representitives there. They also cheered the king for trade and economic gains would boost morale and be beneficial. What the proposed was to allow the king to be leader but only under the council of a parliament of representatives from each tribe. The king smiled and stood proudly and proclaimed he would accept their suggestion and would be willing to work with all. Uzz-ahh then proclaimed that there would be peace again and how the civil wars must stop in order to welcome in progress. Predators that prey upon the weak will be terminated, and if the nations army continues to grow, he proposed a war with the Elves of Laven-ore. This brought cheers from everyone however the Suki delegate stood again. He pointed out how can there be peace if the king was planning wars and hunts of their enemies.

Suto on the third morning arrived at the gorge and was met by his brothers. Happy to see one another the brothers quickly talked of their adventures for hours. Suto explained his plan, but Du-bo criticized him and explained that it was a horrid idea. Traveling through time will be the death of you Suto. Hermit was in agreement. This caused an intense battle between the twins Hermit and Suto. A primal bird arrived amidst the chaos and whispered to Du-bo that the watcher will be in contact soon. Du-bo then pulled his staff with the sphere at the end held it high over his head and slammed it to the ground with an intense beam of golden light scattered about stunning the twins and even caused the ground to quiver. As they collected themselves and stood back up Du-bo informed them of the message from the watcher.

On day three there was a vote on the king's proposal and plan. The majority vote placed the king as ruler of Parlo-5 and the delegates would be appointed to the council to serve in Parliament as a way to have a system of checks and balances. Those who were opposed quickly left and returned to their homelands. King Uz-ahh had an assassin from the Ro tribe take care of the Suki represented. The king tells his advisors to alert the followers and ready the forces to invade the lands of those who were opposed to his vision for the future. The king also called for reinforcements from the Ro, Un-Tak, Khan, and Woot-Woot tribe of Shi-lo. The king received a message from Seedrick high priest of the followers of the great spirit, informing the king that The Great Old One wishes to congratulate the king in person and talk with him on how the followers could be of assistance to the king's grand plan.

Little dose the king knows his life would now be in grave danger from threats of the Hawking-ly, Suki, Tu-va, and an unknown threat from the Followers plot. The Followers of the Great Spirit live on an island off the southern coast of Paradiz-io. Their religion is spreading like wildfires across the southern portion of Paradi-zio. The Great Old One plans on sending missionary's and archeologist to study the ruins and to open education for Parlo-5. However, the Great Old Ones true agenda has yet to be seen. Led by a young and talented bird that goes by the name of Hermes the first expedition takes the missionaries into the land of the beast to a secluded and forgotten ruin and to establish contact with the Forgotten Tribe of Paradi-zio. Hermes was found as an orphan on a hidden expedition to the plain's region of Paradi-zio the great old one noticed Hermes possessed great potential. Hermes and The Great Old ones youngest Daughter Tia have always been close. When Hermes leaves, she awaits eagerly his return, these star-crossed lovers may one day tell the other how they truly feel. When Hermes goes on expeditions, he always sends gifts to Tia. They have quite the collection of antiques and rare items. Tia is nothing like the rest of her family she has no thirst for power and deceit. She rather explores the world with Hermes and leave Follower City to see the nations of the south and east on Parlo-5.

The sky is right the air feels charged while the followers gather on the island of Cu-na-da. The Great Old one proclaims the time is right we must go and spread the word. They must search for the power spheres and perform a ritual that would change Parlo-5. So, across the globe allies of the followers and teams of recruits as well as missionaries set out to find the surviving power spheres. The Great Old One carries a staff with the head of a Derpy leader who went by the name of kallah. In the forehead of this skull is a power crystal from the volcano on Kit-Un. Little is known about the Great Old One, he is a bit of an enigma. It is said he comes from Kit-un and was exiled for his thirst for power and practices of the dark arts. The Tu-Va now resides at the base of the volcano. Though there are other places one can find the gems throughout Parlo-5 he obsesses over eliminating the TU-Va and searching the volcano.

It is early in the morning and primal bird sends a message to Du-bo to go to the canyon rim and await the arrival of the Watcher. Du-bo and the watcher discuss much in this meeting, Du-bo expresses his concern about Suto and the state of the planet with King Uz-ahh in power and supported by a devious parliament. The watcher explains that Suto must go on the search for the crown, and Hermit must go to the island of the great tower and meet with the elders there. Hermit must find his faith again. With the three brothers in possession of power spheres and relics together they would be unstoppable but first they must do as the watcher says before they are ready to face the hidden evil. The watcher explains how they have not been able to see who is the cause of the chaos and even the recent political events that have occurred. the watcher informed Du-bo of the assassination of the Suki delegate and that in the other continents tension and war would soon break out. The watcher informs Du-bo that he is to go to Shi-lo and explore sacred and forgotten places. There Du-bo will come into his own and the three brothers will be ready to fulfill their destiny.

The followers have set out in teams across the globe many have turned up nothing but Hermes and the team trudging through the land of the beast have found many relics and have encountered the forgotten tribe. The forgotten tribe was thought to be extinct but the flourish their numbers are not that of the other tribes on Paradi-zio but they are a force to be reckoned with. They have co-existed with a variety of creatures and beast. Hermes explains why the group is there the tribal leader of the forgotten tribe listens intently. He denies Hermes the access to an old temple in the jungle that they were to leave before the suns rise the next day. Hermes politely agrees and tells the others and they return to Cu-na-da to tell their superiors of their experience in the jungle nation. When Seedrick learns of the encounter he smiles and tells Hermes he did good. Seedrick has one of his disciples ready a force to go in and irradicate the forgotten tribe once they perform an important ritual to aid in their cause. Seedrick, Cera and the Great Old One gather with some decuples in a circle and began chanting and whistling. The smoke from their fire changed colors the 4 spheres they have begun to glow and spirits began to speak from the smoke.

That night King Uz-ahh announces during his state of the union more of his agenda and plans and introduces the members of Parliament. Little dose the king know that this would be his last speech. After the state of the union address the king is to meet with The Great Old One. Uz-ahh sits on his throne with sphere in hand it glowing bright images begin to form inside the sphere. These images are seeming to be premonitions of the king's death. The king becomes overwhelmed with a feeling of sickness. He slides to the floor from his chair and standing before him are the followers of the great spirit. The Great Old One calls for the royal guards. King Uz-ahh was now with spirit, the cause of death at this time is unknown. The next day Parliament announces a vote a vote that establishes power to Seedrick to rule under the council of the parliament. At the ceremony for the king not many spoke but the leader of the nomadic tribes gave a eulogy that moved everyone in attendance. "The king" he said, had a vision of a united Parlo-5 his intentions were pure no matter what some of you thought of him. Now the king has moved on to the next life may he rest in peace and may those of us still here strive to bring the kings vision into reality.

The Hermit, Suto and Du-bo set off on their journeys once again. The Hermit is the first to leave camp. As he is walking along the canyon rim, he hears his name be called from a fog bank. He cannot see anything due to the fog but it is clearly his name being called. He stops and ready's his staff and sphere. Hermit has always been able to communicate with spirits and it would appear there are spirits trying to get his attention now. Then through the fog images begin to form and silhouettes appear. They warn him that the brothers must accomplish what they have been chosen to do. That the future is in peril. They tell Hermit that once he gets to the island to seek out Ida-fa an ancient elder and possibly the oldest on the Parlo-5. Suto sets out to search for the boy king and to learn more. By each day Suto becomes more and more obsessed with time travel and mythical items made by the Maker. Du-bo sits by the fire in the early morning light and is overcome with a vision. It is a shamain he sees a female named Nok. Du-bo in disbelief and confusion calls out to her but she vanishes. Scratching his head, he ventures out of the gorge heading south where eventually he will end up on Shi-lo.

The followers gather once again in their temple on Cu-na-da they now have five spheres and have them arranged. The Great Old One announces the time is right that in three days they will perform an ancient ritual that will rid Parlo-5 of the plague, drought and famine. Then when the stars are right, they would perform the ritual of rituals one that will change the planet forever. Seedrick now in power on Paradi-zio, Cera is furious and overcome with jealousy that Seedrick was chosen over her. The High Priestess, Tia and Cera's mother consuls her daughter while Tia goes to meet Hermes who is stopping in follower city. In Hermes most recent message to Tia he mentioned he had much to tell her. Tia hopes it is a proposal to marry and she daydreams of what it would be like to finally be with the love of her life. When Hermes arrives, he has a flower in his mouth. A beautiful red flower and he gives it to Tia and explains he picked it from the plains. While in the plain region Hermes saw a band of nomads and thought he may have seen his mother. Though excited deep down she was let down that it wasn't a proposal. Tia begins to speak but Hermes begins rambling again about some of the items he has found and he hands Tia a necklace with a beautiful glowing gem. She squeals she loves it; she begins to tell Hermes once again how she feels and she is interrupted for a messenger was sent to tell Hermes that he was to return to Cu-na-da to share what he learned from the most recent expedition.

King Val of the Hawking-ly summons his sons, Tutor and Hero but Tutors' whereabouts are still unknown and Hero and what few survivors of his army set out to go to his father's side. It would seem King Val had succumbed to the same fate as his rival and nemesis King Uz-ahh. By the time Hero arrives it is too late his father has moved on to spirit. Hero weeps and vows to avenge his father's death and find his brother.

With the plagues, famine, and drought over Seedrick gains much approval from all over Paradi-io. The next challenge is to invade the few tribes that still refuse to join the cause. Seedrick performs a meditation ritual to seek guidance. He is unaware of a threat coming from within to over throw him from the throne. Cera is more and more like her father by the day. Her thirst for power and knowledge is never ending and her desire to take over the throne is strong. Cera questions her father on his decision he boldly puts her in her place. He then turned to her and let her in on more of his plans. The Great Old One seeks to travel along with his teams of missionary's and he will send Cera and a team to go into the jungle and explore the ruins and the forgotten temple that they were previously denied access to. She smiles and squeals with joy, and quickly returns to her chambers. Tia and Hermes are walking and Hermes tells her the tale of a Butterfly leader named Yug-soth and a snail with much knowledge known as Goth. Goth is among the oldest creatures on Parlo-5, Hermes hopes that Goth can tell him about his past and where his family are and even what tribe he hails from. Tia understands Hermes desire to connect with his family but she is still hesitant for he is so wrapped up on his adventures and the quest for his family she stops herself from trying to get his attention to tell him her true feelings.

Hermit crosses a hill and finds a light post radiating an intense glow, he is approximately a cycle away from the coast. Once he gets to the coast, he will travel 500miles east to the island of the great tower. At one time there were five great towers that acted as bacons for travelers. Hermit encounters the watcher again. The watcher stresses to Hermit to seek the council of Ida-Fa and to take her a gift to gain her trust. Hermit confused begins to question but the watcher is already gone. Hermit lights a fire and begins to meditate as day turns to dusk. Hermit is curios to what he could offer as a gift for the oldest being on Parlo-5. Hermit had learned of Ida-Fa was direct descendent from the ak-ashi-kowie. Once was the wife of The Bearded One, leader of the Kri. As he sits and ponders all of this, he has a vision, he will offer his dream catcher to Ida-Fa.

Seedrick has his forces ready and sends them out to irradicate the Hawking-ly, Derpy, Suki and Izzo. Accusing these tribes of heir icy and treason against the throne. Cera and her team begin their search of the jungle and The Great Old one plots his next move. Cera and her forces encounters a large beast like creature. The creature speaks and warns them to turn back now and never to return. Cera who has a power sphere wields it high and strikes the beast with a lightning bolt while her legions drive spears in the sides of the great beast. There are many dangers and challenges in the forest. Some of Ceras men have turned up missing and as they carry on the arrive at the temple and are met by the Forgotten tribe. Alongside the forgotten ones are beast, dragons and other creatures which reenforce the army. The battle wages on. Spells, smoke and bodies all around. Cera puts down here sphere and convinces the guards to allow her to be a prisoner that she could be valuable to them. Sha-ki leader of the forgotten ones talks with Cera she explains that she must be allowed to explore the temple and retrieve the scrolls hcr father asked for. Sha-ki and Cera come to an agreement and she is granted access to the temple.

Hermit studies and learns much form Ida-fa she told him of her life experiences and all the changes that has happened over her life time. She hands Hermit a gift a necklace with a power crystal in it. She explained it would be an amplifier that he must go now rondevue with his brothers in the canyon. As he was leaving the last thing Ida-fa said to him was watch the stars you will know when the time is right. Suto has been searching high and low for the boy king. One night in an ancient temple not far from the Suki village his necklace, lantern, and sphere all began to glow. The ground shook then a blinding light happened and he couldn't believe his eyes for standing in front of him was the boy king who looked as if he has never aged. Suto without warning blast the boy king with and energy ball from his sphere. With the boy king stunned Suto explains his task and desire to go back in time. After hearing his story, the boy king said I will trade you the crown for the necklace. Suto agrees to the deal. Now with the crown he heads north to the canyon. Du-Bo is on his way to Shi-Lo when he notices the sky is turning and soon it will be dark. While sitting by the fire Du-Bo has another vision involving Nok. When Nok lived in the Shamain village Du-Bo had a fascination and crush on her. Eventually she would leave but he never got to tell her. Could it be possible Du-Bo thought could it be possible Nok is alive and there is hope for the Shamain species.

When he lands on the beach on Shi-Lo he is greeted by Seiera daughter of the Bearded One. Her and her guards escort Du-Bo to their hidden village. While on their way Seiera tells Du-Bo of the tension and civil wars that are breaking out throughout Shi-Lo and the island nations. Du-Bo asks about Nok, Seiera informs him she knows Nok is alive and last time she saw her she was heading north to the volcano on Shi-Lo. On Shi-Lo there are four main tribes and not a single one gets along with the nearby nations. They fear that the Un-Tak and Ro have teamed up and possibly recruit the Khan and the Kit-Un. The Kri and Shi-Lo have an alliance with Tindogah. While with the Kri Du-Bo learns much about the tribes of the south. He also learns much on the ways and different powers one who possesses a power crystal can do. Hopefully Du-Bo says to himself that it will be enough to stop the threat to Parlo-5.

The stars are right, said The Great Old One the time is right for the ritual. They carefully place the five spheres and gather around the fire. Cera Pulls from a satchel a lantern glowing bright and radiant. The Followers begin their songs and chants. The sky rolls with thunder and lightning, the spheres are radiating and pulsating the ground begins to quake alas the sky opened up and everything went blank. It seems as if a giant catastrophe has happened. Parlo-5 has split into 8 different realms rotating where the planet once stood. A majority of all living things have been wiped out. As they come to, Cera realizes her father has disappeared. and Seedrick consoled her as she wept. The high priestess stood at her side as for the other disciples they didn't make it. As the priestess looks around it looks as if a blast of energy and fall out ravaged everything.

""

Suto arrived at the canyon placed the crown on his head and began a spell then a flash of light came and Suto was gone all that remained was the crown. When The Hermit arrived, he saw few items he recognized as Suto's he began to weep for they were too late the ritual is almost complete. No sign of Du-bo who remains on Shi-Lo searching for crystals and Nok.

The watchers as the awoke flocked to the great tree, shocked and in awe of the sight in the sky that dreadful night were pieces of Parlo-5 floating about. The lands of Parlo have split into nine realms. They quickly realize that it was the Followers responsible for the chaos that had previously plagued the planet. One watcher sent word via primal bird to the Royal watcher whose last whereabouts were in the temples on Du-Bob-Way where he is protected by the birds of Du-Bob-Way.

When he opened his eye Hermes looks around and notices the damage, he is unsure where he is. He sees something coming towards him it is a primal bird that goes by the name of Isaiah. He begins walking what he thinks is east but is still disoriented from the disaster. Hise ears rang his body hurt but he seemed to be otherwise unsaved. In the distance he sees something fluttering about, could it be? Yug-Soth the leader of the butterflies was approaching. Herme thought to himself about his love for Tia and how he hoped she was safe. Yug-Soth landed on Hermes beak, and told Hermes it was nice to see life. Hermes replied that he too thought the same thing when seeing Yug-Soth, he said " there is hope, there will always be hope"

"To Be Continued..."

Printed in the United States
by Baker & Taylor Publisher Services